MW01142085

READY

FOR SOMETHING
NEW!

Date Due

NOV 2 9 1999			
OCT 3 - 2000			
DEC 0 3 2002			

The Standard Publishing Company, Cincinnati, Ohio
A division of Standex International Corporation
© 1993 by The Standard Publishing Company
All rights reserved.
Printed in the United States of America.
00 99 98 97 96 95 94 93   5 4 3 2 1

ISBN 0-7847-0097-4
Cataloging-in-Publication data available

Edited by Diane Stortz
Designed by Coleen Davis

CONTENTS

THE SAME OLD BREAKFAST

Nathan stacked pancakes
on two plates—one for himself,
one for his brother, Matthew.
"Breakfast is ready!"
Nathan called to Matthew.
"Come and get it!"

Matthew poked his pancakes.

"Why do we always
eat pancakes for breakfast?"
he asked.

"I do not want
the same old breakfast anymore.
I am ready for something new."

Nathan crossed his arms.

"Something new?" he said.

"First you say

you want a new breakfast.

Next you will say

you want a new job."

"You are right," said Matthew.

"I do not want

to be a fisherman anymore.

I want

to stretch

and yawn and sing songs

I want to skip stones

on the waves."

8

"But we always go fishing,"

said Nathan.

"We are fishermen."

"*You* are
a fisherman,"

said Matthew.

"*I* want to be

a stone-skipping song singer."

"What is wrong with you?"

asked Nathan.

"Are you sick?"

"I am bored,"

said Matthew.

"I am tired of

the same old breakfast.

I am tired of the same old job.

I am ready for something new."

Nathan waved his arms.

"Something new?" he said.

"First you say

you want a new breakfast.

Then you say you want a new job.

Next you will say

you want a new house."

"You are right,"

said Matthew.

"This house is old.

"The walls have cracks.

The floors have creaks.

Soon we will slide

right off this hill."

Nathan laughed.

"We are safe," he said.

"Our house is built on a rock."

"I know," said Matthew.

"We helped our father

build this house."

"That is right," said Nathan.

"I remember, too."

MATTHEW & NATHAN REMEMBER

One day when Matthew
and Nathan were young,
their father said,
"Come for a walk with me."
Matthew and Nathan
and their father
walked out of the village
and up a tall hill.
"We will build a new house here,"
said Father.
"This is a good spot."

"This is a not
a good spot,"
said Nathan.
"The ground
is too hard
for a garden."

"This is not a good spot,"
said Matthew.
"The hill is too steep to play ball."

Father just smiled.

"This is a good spot," he said.

"This hill is strong.

It will hold our house steady."

17

Matthew and Nathan

and their father worked

for many weeks

to build the house.

Down the hill

they rolled boulders and bushes.

Up the hill

they carried boards and bricks.

"We are wise to build our house
on a rock," said Father.
"This house will last.
You will live here a long time."

19

MATTHEW'S NEW HOUSE

Their father was right.
Matthew and Nathan
had lived in the house
a long time.

"Now I want to live
somewhere new," said Matthew.
"I will build a new house!"

"But we are brothers," said Nathan.
"We have always
lived together."

"We will still be brothers,"
said Matthew. "And we will visit
each other every day. I promise."

"Where will you build
your new house?" asked Nathan.
"Come with me," said Matthew.
"I will show you."

"But what
about breakfast?"
said Nathan. "What about
my beautiful pancakes?"

Matthew shook his head.

"I do not think we can use your pancakes to build my house. They are almost hard enough, but not quite."

Nathan followed Matthew
down the hill to the beach.

Matthew spread his arms wide.

"Ta-dah!" he cried.

"I will build my new house here."

Nathan scrunched his toes

in the wet sand.

"You cannot build a house here,"

he said. "The sand is soft.

Your house will not stand."

Matthew did not listen.

"I will have a beach house,"

he said.

"I will smell the fresh sea air.

I will hear the seagulls call.

I will catch fish

from my bedroom window."

"You will wash away
with the waves," said Nathan.
"You will blow away
with the wind.
Great globs of seaweed
will block your front door."

"Waves do not scare me,"
said Matthew bravely.
"Wind does not scare me."
He looked at the sea.
He chewed on one fingernail.

"Does seaweed really float
in great globs?" he asked.
"I guess we shall find out,"
said Nathan.

The brothers cut boards.

They made bricks

and piled up stones.

They pushed and pulled

and sawed and hammered.

When the house was done,
they put down their tools.

"My new house is beautiful,"
said Matthew.

"Thank you for helping me."

Matthew looked out
his new window.
The waves on the sea
sparkled in the sun.
"Tomorrow we will have a party,"
said Matthew.
"All our friends will come
to my new house."

Nathan looked out
Matthew's new window.
He could see dark clouds
far away.

"A party is a good idea," said Nathan.
"But stay with me tonight.
Your bed is still at our old house.
Your pajamas are there."

The brothers walked

across the beach

and up the hill.

Behind them, dark clouds

drifted closer to the shore.

A storm began at midnight.

Rain splashed and crashed

and slashed

into Nathan's old house.

Wind and thunder shook the walls.

Lightning hit the hill.

Matthew slept through the storm.

But Nathan stood by the window,

looking toward the sea.

MATTHEW'S SURPRISE

Matthew woke up early.

Nathan had fixed pancakes

for breakfast.

Matthew did not eat them.

"Hurry," said Matthew.

"We must go to my new

house. We must get ready

for my party tonight."

39

The brothers walked down the hill.

When they came to the beach,

Matthew's eyes grew big.

He looked up the beach.

He looked down the beach.

"My house!" he cried.

"Where is my new house?

It was here yesterday!"

Nathan felt sad for his brother.

"Maybe we are not

in the right place," he said.

"Maybe your house

is around the bend."

"But here is the path

to the village," said Matthew.

"My house was right here.

Who took it?"

Nathan put an arm

around his brother.

"I think the storm last night took your house," he said.

"Wind blew away the sand.

Waves knocked over the walls.

The stones sank.

The boards floated away.

Your house is gone."

Matthew shook his head sadly.
"My beautiful new house!"
he cried. "And now where
will I live?"

"You will live with me," said
Nathan. "My house is large and
sturdy. It is built on a rock."

"Your house is not new,"

grumped Matthew.

"Your house is our old house."

"We will do new things there,"

said Nathan.

"It will seem like a new house."

The brothers turned
and walked up the hill.
"I will fix another breakfast when
we get home," said Nathan.
"I will fix juicy melon. I will fix
cheese and eggs and mugs of milk."

Matthew smiled.

"I would like that," he said.

"Juicy melon and cheese
and eggs and mugs of milk
will be a fine breakfast
for fishermen like us."

And it was.